Please return this book on or before the date shown above. To renew go to www.essex.gov.uk/libraries, ring 0345 603 7628 or go to any Essex library.

Essex County Council

Chapter Readers

'The Reading Bug'
An original concept by Jenny Moore
© Jenny Moore 2021

Illustrated by Kaley McCabe

Published by MAVERICK ARTS PUBLISHING LTD
Studio 11, City Business Centre, 6 Brighton Road,
Horsham, West Sussex, RH13 5BB
© Maverick Arts Publishing Limited November 2021
+44 (0)1403 256941

A CIP catalogue record for this book is available at the British Library.

ISBN 978-1-84886-848-9

www.maverickbooks.co.uk

This book is rated as: Grey Band (Guided Reading)

The Reading Bug

Written by
Jenny Moore

Illustrated by
Kaley McCabe

Chapter 1

Sam and Ravi couldn't wait for the summer holidays. Six whole weeks of freedom, starting with a sleepover in Sam's back garden! They just had to get through the boring end-of-term assembly first. The headmaster was droning on about doing lots of reading over the holidays.

Reading? thought Sam. *We do enough of that at school. Why would I want to spend my summer holidays stuck in a book when I could be having fun?* There certainly wouldn't be any reading at the sleepover! He and Ravi would be too busy watching superhero cartoons and eating sweets and chocolate. Sam's mouth watered at the thought of all those sugary treats.

"Psst!" He nudged Ravi with his elbow. "Did I tell you I've got a giant pack of Fizzy Raspberry Rockets for tonight?" he whispered. "Plus three tubes of Cola Chew-Chews and four Chocolate Caramel Frogs. What about you? What are you going to bring?"

"I've still got some of those Sherbet Explosions my dad got me from America," Ravi whispered back. "And Mum's bought me a huge bag of popcorn and some of those new pizza-flavoured crisps."

"Pizza crisps? Wow, they sound awesome," said Sam. "I can't wait to try them. We need to decide what cartoons we're going to watch too. How about—?" But Sam didn't get to finish the sentence. He was interrupted by a stern '*shush*' from their teacher.

"Stop talking you two, and listen," she said. "Mrs Page has kindly given up her time to come and talk to us. The least you can do is listen politely."

"Mrs Page?" Sam repeated. "Who's she?"

"She's the new librarian at the town library," said his teacher. "You'd know that if you were listening."

Sam glanced back to the front of the hall. The headmaster had finished talking now, and a lady in a bright green blouse was holding up a poster about the Summer Reading Challenge.

That must be Mrs Page, Sam thought, wondering why she looked so familiar. She had dark hair tied up in a bun, and funny round glasses that made her eyes look really big—like bug eyes! Sam was sure he'd seen her

somewhere before. But it couldn't be the library because he never went there!

"That sounds great, thank you Mrs Page," said the headmaster. "Hopefully we'll all be bitten by the reading bug this summer!"

Mrs Page blushed. "Well, er... yes," she said, suddenly lost for words. "I certainly hope we'll have lots of new reading fans anyway. Please do come along to the library and sign up for the Summer Reading Challenge, everyone. It's going to be such fun."

Huh, thought Sam. *A whole holiday reading books? That doesn't sound like much fun to me!*

Chapter 2

Sam finished his dinner in record time. He couldn't wait to get out into the garden and set up camp for the night in the new tent. It looked amazing! But Ravi still had half a jacket potato left to eat. He was smiling politely as Sam's little sister, Gina, chattered on about the Summer Reading Challenge and how she couldn't wait to get started.

Less smiling and more chewing, thought Sam, willing his friend to hurry up.

"I met Mrs Page when I popped into the library this morning," said Sam's mum. "She seems very nice. It turns out she's moved into Mr Kay's old house down the road."

Of course, thought Sam. *That's why she looked so familiar.* He remembered seeing the removal van full of boxes marked BOOKS when she moved in.

"It might be nice if you signed up for the Summer Reading Challenge too, Sam," said his mum." Seeing as Mrs Page is one of our neighbours now."

Sam pulled a face. "I'd rather do a Summer *Watching* Challenge! I'd challenge myself to watch every single episode of *Team Superhero*. That would be cool."

"Ooh yes," agreed Ravi. "That would be brilliant. We could go back and watch them all, right from the start. Do you remember that one where Mind Magic got kidnapped by the Blue Bandit and put in the brain-wiping machine? And his butler had to save him?"

"Yes," said Sam. "I love that one. Mind Magic is my favourite of all the superheroes. Imagine travelling round the world, fighting crime, just using the power of your mind. Without ever having to leave the comfort of your luxury superhero headquarters!"

Ravi's eyes gleamed. "If I had my own private butler bringing me chocolate bars on a tray, I'd never want to leave headquarters either!"

"We should watch some Mind Magic episodes of *Team Superhero* tonight," said Sam.

"And some Super Suction ones," added Ravi. "He's *my* favourite. I like the episode where he and The Hooked Claw have a fight halfway up the Eiffel Tower."

Sam's mum smiled at them. "I'm happy for you to borrow my tablet to watch them on, but don't forget about the 'sleep' bit of the sleepover. I don't want you watching cartoons all night and being tired tomorrow."

"We won't," replied Sam, winking at Ravi.

"And if you get too cold or scared out there you can always come back to the house," Sam's mum added. "I've made up the camp bed for you in Sam's room, just in case," she told Ravi.

Ravi smiled his politest smile. "Thank you," he said.

Sam's reaction wasn't quite as polite though. "Scared?!" he snorted, spraying a mouthful of blackcurrant squash all over the table. "Of course we won't be scared. What's there to be scared of in the back garden?"

Chapter 3

Camping out in the new tent was just as good as Sam had imagined. Once he and Ravi had crawled inside, they were in their own secret world. It was just the two of them now, plus an assortment of bugs who seemed to have set up camp alongside them. Sam wasn't bothered by creepy crawlies though. He didn't mind if the local spiders and woodlice wanted to watch *Team Superhero* with them, as long as they kept away from the food!

"I love this episode," said Ravi, as the theme music started up. "It's the one where Super Suction gets stuck halfway up that skyscraper."

"Ooh yes, that's a good one," agreed Sam, happily.

He'd loved every episode they'd seen so far. Watching cartoons on Mum's tablet, while filling his mouth with crisps, popcorn and sweets, was the perfect start to the summer holidays!

"Don't let me eat any more Fizzy Raspberry Rockets though," added Ravi. "My tongue feels all tingly and my tummy hurts."

"Don't worry, the Raspberry Rockets are all gone," said Sam, glancing down at the pile of empty wrappers. "In fact, that's *all* the food gone, by the looks of it."

"Oh no," said Ravi as the tablet screen went black. "That's the end of cartoon-watching as well. I think the battery must have died. I guess that means it's time for the 'sleep' bit of the sleepover."

"I suppose so," agreed Sam, checking his watch. It was gone midnight. He didn't feel very sleepy though. His head was still buzzing from all the sugar. "It's a pity we don't have Mind Magic's powers," he said, as he wriggled down inside his sleeping bag. "Then we could travel to the sitting room using the power of our minds and watch cartoons on the television instead!"

"I wish I had Super Suction's powers," said Ravi. "I'd like to climb up Big Ben and the Empire State Building. Or maybe the Leaning Tower of Pisa." He pointed to a tall leaning shadow on the tent wall and laughed. "Your washing line post looks a bit like the Leaning Tower of Pisa with the moon shining behind it!"

Sam laughed too. "Yes, I see what you mean. You can tell it's a full moon tonight—it's so bright." He thought for a moment. "Climbing tall towers *would* be really cool but I'd still rather have Mind Magic's powers, I think. I'd love to be able to travel anywhere in the whole world without leaving my chair."

"Where would you go, then?" asked Ravi. "If you could go anywhere?"

Sam unzipped his sleeping bag with a sigh. "Right now I'd choose the frozen wastes of Outer Icelandica from the werewolf episode, just to cool off a bit! Mum needn't have worried about us being too cold. It's boiling in here!"

"The werewolves would put me off," said Ravi. "And I *really* wouldn't like to get on the wrong side of that werewalrus, or those killer gulls! Did you see how sharp their beaks were?" He shuddered at the thought. "I'd *hate* to meet one of those."

Chapter 4

Sam had finally dropped off to sleep when something sharp jabbed him in the ribs. *Ow!* It was Ravi's elbow! "Wake up," Ravi hissed.

Sam jolted up into a sitting position. "What is it? What's wrong?"

"There's something flying around outside the tent," said Ravi. He pointed to a pair of dark swooping shadows on the tent wall. "What if it's killer gulls?"

Sam laughed. "Don't be silly, they're only in cartoons."

"Well if they're not killer gulls, what are they then?" asked Ravi. He still sounded scared.

"Probably just bats," said Sam, drowsily. "We get a lot of them round here in the summer." He rolled over and closed his eyes.

HOWWWL!

Sam was jolted awake again, some time later, by a strange noise coming from the end of the garden.

HOWWWWL!

There it was again! Sam sat up and stared in horror at the shadow moving across the tent wall. It wasn't bats this time. This shadow was huge and hulking, towering over the top of the garden wall. It was a giant monster of a shadow!

Ravi was fast asleep and snoring now. But not for long.

"Ravi!" Sam shook his friend's sleeping bag. "Wake up! You have to see this!"

"Wharrr?" came the sleepy reply. Ravi sat up and rubbed his eyes, but the shadow had already moved on.

"Did you see it?" asked Sam.

Ravi looked confused. "See what?"

"That enormous shadow prowling along the back lane! It looked like a monster!"

Ravi shook his head. "I must have missed it, sorry. Are you sure it wasn't a dream?"

Sam pulled his hoodie on over his pyjama top. "It wasn't a dream," he said. "I was wide awake. There was a horrible howling noise—two howls in fact—and then a huge shadow looming right across the tent. It was enormous. Like a monster!"

Ravi shivered. "What sort of monster?" he asked. "A werewolf? A werewalrus?"

"I don't know for sure," said Sam. "But we'll soon find out. Come on, grab your hoodie and let's go."

Chapter 5

Sam unzipped the tent and scrambled out into the moonlit night, with Ravi close behind. They stopped to put on their trainers and then tore off down the garden towards the bottom gate. It opened out onto a narrow alleyway that ran along the backs of all the houses on Sam's street.

"It can't have got far," said Sam, dodging round the neighbour's bins.

"No, not if it's a werewalrus," agreed Ravi. "They're not very fast out of water."

But it wasn't a werewalrus *or* a werewolf. The boys swung out of the end of the lane and gasped out loud.

There it was.

A bug, as big as a fully-grown man, scuttled along the pavement on its back legs. It looked like a giant woodlouse, with enormous feelers that waved in the night air.

"Wow!" said Ravi, staring in amazement. "It really *is* a monster."

"Or an alien," said Sam. "It must have come to check out Planet Earth and report back to the other bug-aliens back home, before they decide whether or not to invade."

"An alien invasion?" Ravi gulped. "Like in *Team Superhero* you mean? The one with Mind Magic and the Martians?"

"Exactly," said Sam. "We need to find out what it's planning. Come on, let's follow it and see where it goes."

The boys followed the giant bug past the church, round the roundabout and on into the town centre.

It stopped outside the pub and swung round, its feelers wiggling in the night air.

"Get back!" hissed Sam, pulling Ravi into the shadows. They ducked down behind the recycling bins and held their breath.

"Do you think it saw us?" whispered Ravi after a while.

"I don't know," said Sam, trying not to think about big bug pincers reaching round the side of the bins in search of a late night snack. "I hope not."

His heart was beating like crazy as he peered out. But the coast was clear.

"It's alright, it's heading for Fore Street," he said.

"Maybe it wants to look in the shops while everyone's asleep," joked Ravi. "Or maybe it's going to the garage to pick up some spare parts for its spacecraft."

But the alien bug headed straight past the shops without a second glance. And it didn't turn right at the crossroads towards the garage. It turned left, instead, towards the town hall and the library.

"Maybe it's come to sign up for Mrs Page's Summer Reading Challenge," said Sam, with a smile. "It's going to have a long wait though. The library won't be open for hours!"

He'd only meant it as a joke. But the bug really *did* seem to be heading for the library. It stopped in front of the window, as if it was admiring the children's book display, and let out a long alien howl. And then, much to the boys' surprise, it pulled a set of keys out from under its shell and let itself in through the library door.

Chapter 6

"Woah!" said Sam. "What's an alien bug doing with keys to our library? This is getting *seriously* weird now."

"What should we do?" asked Ravi. "Should we follow it inside? What if it's dangerous?"

"I don't know," said Sam. Trailing behind the bug at a safe distance was one thing. That felt like an exciting adventure. Following it inside a deserted library seemed much more risky. What if it spotted them? What if it attacked them with its giant bug fangs? If only they had magic mind-travelling powers like Mind Magic. They could use their minds to carry on their spying operation, while their bodies stayed safely outside, away from harm.

But magical mind travel only worked in superhero cartoons.

Sam pulled himself up tall, trying to make himself feel braver. He and Ravi might not be *super*heroes, but this was their chance to be heroes all the same. If the town (and the planet) really were in danger, they couldn't stand by and do nothing.

Ravi looked scared too. "We could just call the police," he suggested, "and let them take over from here."

Sam shook his head. "No, they'd never believe us. Not without proper evidence. Besides, by the time we get to a phone it might have gone again. We need to catch that bug ourselves, and then they'll know we're not making it up."

"OK," said Ravi. "I guess you're right. I wish my legs would stop shaking though."

"You'll be fine," said Sam, sounding more confident than he felt. "There's two of us and only one of it. And the bug hasn't spotted us yet, which means we've got the element of surprise on our side. As long as we stick together, we'll be alright."

Sam pushed open the library door as quietly as he could, and they crept inside.

Chapter 7

The bug was standing by the fiction shelves, pulling out one book after another and adding them to a growing pile on the floor. Every time it found a new book it liked, it made funny clicks of excitement by rubbing its feelers together.

It seemed to have stopped howling though.

The boys crept closer, hiding behind a shelf of cookery books. Sam peered round the library, looking for something they could use to help them catch it. His gaze fell on the Summer Reading Challenge display. It was a different poster to the one Mrs Page had brought into assembly. This one said 'Catch Yourself a Fresh Adventure', and there was a big fishing net next to it on the display table. Perfect!

"I've got a plan," he whispered to Ravi. He pointed to the net. "We'll sneak up from behind and throw that net over its head before it can get away. And then once we've caught it, we'll ring the police on the library phone and tell them there's been a break-in. They'll *have* to come and investigate then."

Ravi nodded. "Alright," he agreed. "Let's do it."

They tiptoed across to the Reading Challenge display while the bug was choosing its next book. So far so good. They grabbed hold of the net and stretched it out between them. It was nice and strong, and just the right size for catching giant bugs.

Click, click, click, went the bug's feelers as it pulled out another book.

"After three," whispered Sam. "One... Two... Three!"

The boys charged over to the fiction shelf and threw the net at the unsuspecting bug.

It worked! The net dropped down over its big buggy head and shoulders and tangled round its feelers. The bug let out a horrified shriek, twisting round in surprise. It wriggled and squirmed, lashing out at the netting with its head.

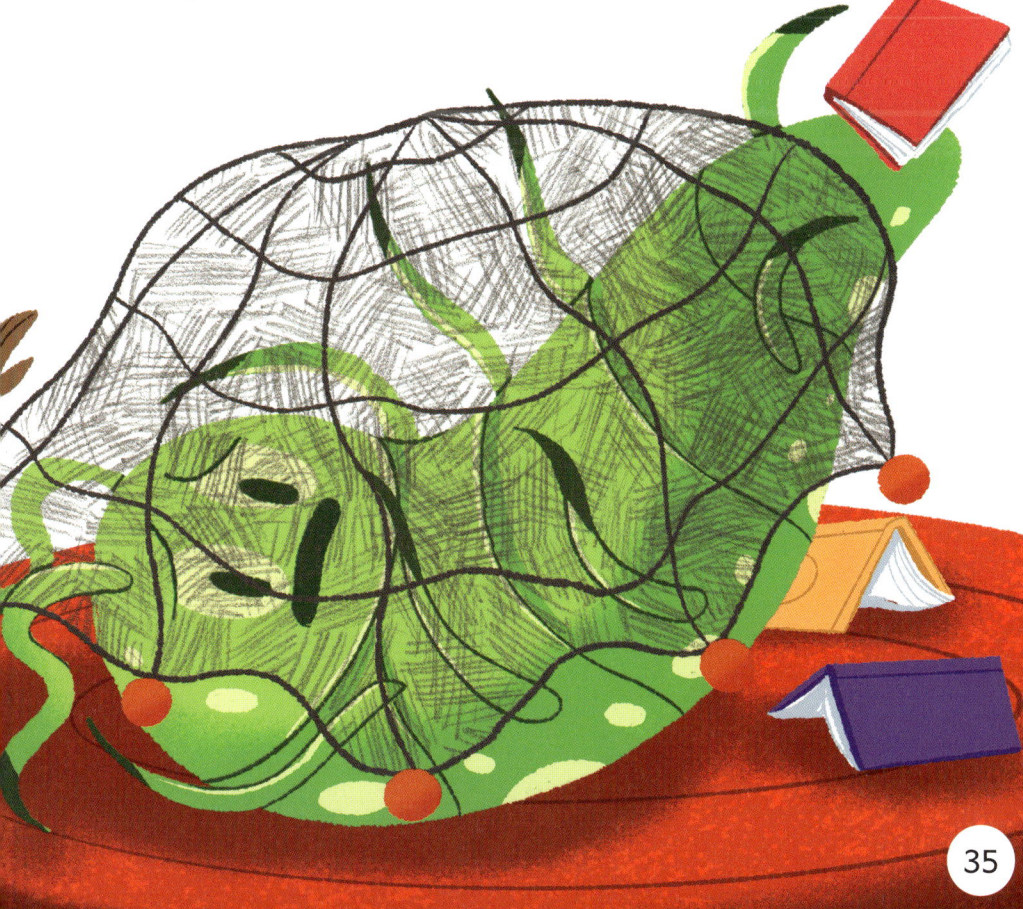

Sam felt a strange, tingly tickle as the bug's jaws caught the back of his hand. He whipped his arm back in surprise, dropping his side of the net. Ravi dropped his side of the net too, staring at the back of his hand in surprise. "Ooh, that tingles," he said.

The bug seized its chance, wriggling its body clear, and staggering across the library with the net still tangled round its feelers.

Sam and Ravi glanced at each other. What now? The bug seemed strangely frightened, backing away from them as if *they* were the scary alien life forms. But before either of them could speak a large cloud passed in front of the moon and the bug began to change shape.

Chapter 8

The boys watched in fascinated horror as the bug's feelers pulled back inside its head and its shell began to shrink. Maybe it wasn't an alien after all. Maybe it was the bug version of a werewolf, that only transformed into a bug in the light of a full moon. Did that mean it was turning back to its human form, now that the moon was hidden by the clouds?

Horror turned to amazement as the bug took its new shape in front of them. It was Mrs Page, the librarian! She pushed her funny bug glasses back up her nose and gave the boys an embarrassed smile.

"Ah, hello there," she said. "I hope I didn't frighten you."

Sam was lost for words.

"Wh-wh-what just happened?" stammered Ravi. "We thought you were an alien, checking out the planet to see if your alien bug people should invade or not."

"An alien? Bless me, no," laughed Mrs Page. "I'm just a regular Earth librarian. I was bitten by a reading bug when I was your age and now I change into one too. It's only once a year though, on the first full moon in July. It's quite good fun really. I can walk up walls and crawl upside-down on the ceiling!"

"Wow!" said Ravi. "Just like Super Suction! That's so cool!"

"And I'd never hurt anyone," added Mrs Page. She looked at them and blushed. "Apart from the odd little bite when someone comes too close, maybe. I'm sorry if I nipped you by mistake."

Sam remembered the strange tingly feeling in his hand from earlier. He glanced down to see a funny red mark on his skin, shaped like an open book.

Ravi was staring at *his* hand as well. "Does this mean I'll turn into a giant bug once every July as well?" he asked, looking worried. But then his face broke into a grin. "And does that mean I'll be able to climb up walls, like Super Suction?"

Mrs Page nodded. "You will when you transform, yes. But there's much more to being a reading bug than that. The main thing you'll notice is how hungry you are for fresh books to read. You won't be able to get enough of them. And *that* lasts all year round."

Her eyes grew large and dreamy behind their glasses. "Books are amazing," she said. "They're like mind portals. I can curl up with a book in my sitting room and travel to all sorts of exciting new places. I get to have the most incredible adventures without ever leaving my armchair!"

"Like Mind Magic!" the boys said together.

Chapter 9

The boys promised to keep Mrs Page's secret, and she promised not to tell anyone that they'd been chasing her round town in the middle of the night.

"I'm sorry again about the whole biting thing," she said, as they said their goodbyes at Sam's garden gate. "I really didn't mean to."

"That's okay," said Sam. "Being a reading bug sounds cool!" He was about to add 'apart from the reading bit' but something stopped him. He glanced at the pile of books in Mrs Page's arms and felt a strange tug inside his chest. They *did* look pretty good. If he wasn't so tired he might have been tempted to borrow one himself.

"I can't wait!" agreed Ravi. "Hopefully there won't be any clouds to cover the moon next year. I don't want to change back into a human halfway up the clock tower!"

"Just be careful," warned Mrs Page. "And don't let anyone see you," she added, as she trotted off down the lane, clutching her precious books to her chest.

It was much cooler in the tent when they got back inside.

"What a night," said Sam, snuggling down into his sleeping bag. "That beats anything on *Team Superhero*!"

"Yes," agreed Ravi, with a big yawn. "Best sleepover *ever!*"

★★★

The boys slept in late the next morning. They were still fast asleep when Sam's mum came to fetch them for breakfast.

"Come on sleepyheads, up you get," she called. "I've made pancakes."

The boys sat up and rubbed their eyes.

"I had the strangest dream last night," said Ravi. "About Mrs Page turning into a giant bug!"

Sam stared at him in disbelief. "Me too!" he said. "And we tried to catch her with a net in the library and then she bit us."

Ravi nodded. "Yes, that's what happened in my dream too. How strange! It must have been all those sweets we ate last night!"

"Must have been," agreed Sam. "Or maybe it was all those videos we watched." He glanced down at his hand, remembering the strange bite mark in his dream. But there was nothing there now. Of course there wasn't!

He carried his mum's tablet back to the house and sat down at the breakfast table with Ravi. His stomach rumbled at the smell of pancakes.

"I thought you boys would be hungry after a whole night out there in the cold," said his mum. "So tuck in, both of you. We've already had ours. And then I'm going to take your sister down to the library to sign up for the

Summer Reading Challenge."

Sam felt a strange tug in his chest. "The library?" he repeated. "Can we come? I really want to get some books out." He thought of all the amazing stories waiting to be discovered and his heart beat a little faster. Maybe it *hadn't* all been a dream after all.

"Me too," said Ravi. "I want to spend the whole day reading."

Sam's mum looked at them in surprise. "Really?" she said. "When did you two get the reading bug?"

The boys shrugged.

"Who knows?" said Sam, with a sly wink at his friend.

"It's a mystery," agreed Ravi, winking back.

Discussion Points

1. Why does Sam not want to take part in the Reading Challenge at first?

2. Who is Sam's new neighbour?
a) Mrs Page
b) Ravi
c) Gina

3. What was your favourite part of the story?

4. Where did the boys catch the Reading Bug?

5. Why do you think the boys suddenly had the urge to read at the end?

6. Who was your favourite character and why?

7. There were moments in the story when Sam and Ravi had to **investigate**. Where do you think the story shows this most?

8. What do you think happens after the end of the story?

Book Bands for Guided Reading

The Institute of Education book banding system is a scale of colours that reflects the various levels of reading difficulty. The bands are assigned by taking into account the content, the language style, the layout and phonics. Word, phrase and sentence level work is also taken into consideration.

The Maverick Readers Scheme is a bright, attractive range of books covering the pink to grey bands. All of these books have been book banded for guided reading to the industry standard and edited by a leading educational consultant.

To view the whole Maverick Readers scheme, visit our website at

www.maverickearlyreaders.com

Or scan the QR code to view our scheme instantly!

Maverick Chapter Readers
(From Lime to Grey Band)

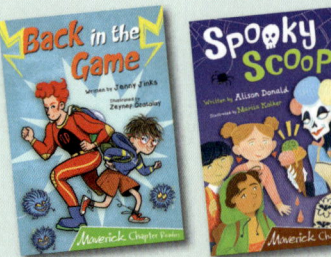